Waldmunt

Lindsey Brenton

Dedicated to my husband. May I continue to write lullabies for you.

Waldmunt

Through the wicked forest

Past the dying trees

A large mansion I see

Crouch by the stream

Wash your sinful hands and feet

Praying the master of the house

Is more charitable than me

Walking up to the double doors

I knock knock knock

The only sound, so forlorn

I pray that the color is gone from my hands

When the door opens

And before me stands a man

His eyes are dark

As is his hair

And he asks me

"What are you doing here?"

"I ask not for much, please sir

Just a place to rest my head,

And if you have extra clothes,

I would be forever in your debt."

He looks at me with curious eyes

Before looking down at my tattered feet

"A woman like you is trouble, ma'am.

And trouble will have none of me.

Stay an evening, I will lend you clothes and shoes

However, when the morrow comes

And the sky changes hues

I want you out of my sight

Not a word of complaint from you."

I nod, as what else is a woman to do?

He lets me cross his threshold

Politely bowing my head

Wishing I were a better sight

Than in a muddy, tattered dress

"What is the name of my guest?"

He asks

And I hesitate to say

For a name is the very thing

That had me out in such straights

On this day

"Call me Miss Waldmunt, good sir.

And what is your name, I pray?"

He eyes me with suspicion

Before nodding his head

"Call me Bartholomew, most esteemed guest."

Bartholomew

The woman here, in my home

Would prefer to be alone

Which I have no qualms with

For I live somewhere secret

Where not even animals

Dare to roam

I take her to a bedroom

Find her a new dress

And let the lady sit in peace

For I am no hostess

And she would not constitute as a guest

However, I am not without manners

And I try to work on dinner

For what man in the world

Would let a lady go without supper?

Waldmunt

What a gloomy night

What horrors make up life

What could I do to make it right?

What is living but a strife?

What do you live for if not spite?

What happened to my hunting knife?

Waldmunt

My father wanted a son

He made that abundantly clear

Instead he got me

And my sister dear

He made sure we knew the ways of the world

So we'd never live in fear

But here I am, and there she is

How the gods of misfortune must sneer

At the stupid little people

Who would try to persevere

Bartholomew

I knock upon the door

Of her temporary chambers

Speaking through the wood

That our dinner is served

She calls out an excuse

And I'm sure she just wants to be alone

That is fine

As I want none of her

But I am still a man

Who never forgets his manners

I call through the door

Letting her know what's for supper

And down the hall I go

To eat all alone

Ne'er does this place get visitors

Though I am not lonely

I have my own demons

My own problems

To keep my mind company

Though as my mind wanders

As I sit down to eat

I can't help but wonder

What made a woman like that

Come to my home

I suppose I should take this chance

To not be completely alone

At least for a moment

Perhaps I should have offered

Her to stay longer

What are the chances she would like it here

When I am not the only ghost in these halls?

Perhaps I should take

Any chance at all

For company

When the servants left

And my father died,

Perhaps accepting this is how things are

Is all just a lie

Perhaps-

"Excuse me?"

I look up and there she is

The woman who goes by Waldmunt

"Sorry I took so long, sir.

As you can see I have seen better days.

The clothes you supplied will suffice,

Though they look as if they were from Shakespeare plays."

I chuckle at that

From her dry wit

Though I see her point

As the clothes are out of style and out of date

And layered in a bit of grime.

"I apologize."

I say

"There have been no ladies in this home

For quite a long time.

If there were something better here

I swear I would offer it."

Waldmunt walks to the window

She then turns to me

Her face a bit uncertain

"Do you have any extra curtains?"

I blink, surprised at her request

And without thinking she pulls the fabric

Across her chest

The old drapes are red and gold

They have been here longer than I,

They are so old

"Do the clothes I have provided truly vex you so?"

Waldmunt walks to the table

Though I know her thoughts are elsewhere

She sits and looks at me

"Yes." She says

Waldmunt

The clothes I wear itch

They smell

And so I must scratch

And hold my breath

Before dinner I didn't even have time

To take a bath

The mud cakes my legs

And they itch as well

I eye the curtains

The material was soft

But I cannot worsen

My relationship with my host

Perhaps if I'm lucky

After he turns me away in the morning

I can sneak back inside his home

And hopefully he won't notice me

I can live in the attic and quietly roam

The empty halls of the manor

Until I come to a better understanding

Of what my life is to be

And what I must do next

My host, Bartholomew watches me

Not yet saying a word about the drapery

I notice a platter at my spot at the table

Sitting in my designated place

The table is long and I can't help but notice

He is staring down the curtains

With a hint of a grimace

I look at the platter and lift the lid

Seeing that dinner is a simple meal

Of some sort of meat

With carrots and potatoes in stew

I look back up at him

He looks at me

And I finally notice

A lack of other human beings

No servants or help or even family

It is just the two of us

Just him and me

Bartholomew stands, walking slowly

To the curtains

He extends his hand

And rips the curtains from the wall

I scream in surprise

And the fabric covers him

For a moment he is a monster

Of red and crimson

He wrestles his way out

I sit at my chair

Watching him, wary

For a man who destroys so easily

Is not to be trusted without reason

I wonder silently if I should apologize

If perhaps my inquiry

Could be seen as such an insult in his eyes

That perhaps he tore down the drapes

Just to frighten me

Bartholomew turns and holds up

The shimmering fabric

That I just moments ago wanted to adorn

In place of the rags I was given

He observes the fabric calmly

Before stating very simply

"It is dusty, and old, but a few shakes will fix it

After dinner I'll free it of dust

But, I have to ask, how do you plan to make it a garment?"

Heart wildly beating,

I clear my throat to tell him

"Some strategic folding and wrapping

And perhaps a pin or something

Could hold it

Or, perhaps, would you happen to have a sewing kit?"

He folds it up before sitting back down

Setting the curtain by his side

Taking the lid off his platter

He is silent while he starts to frown

"I believe I do. Somewhere."

And that was that, we sit and eat

In near perfect silence

Until I look at my host and ask

"Excuse me, what is this meat?"

Bartholomew

I beat the curtains out the window

Watching dust fly up and dissipate

Every beating of the stick

Lightening the weight

And I wonder how many years

Have been lost in the drapes

What stories could objects tell?

If they could speak

Would I have to kill them as well?

Waldmunt

Lying in the bath

Scrubbing my arms and feet

I scrub until the water is black

And I can't see my body underneath

Dinner was fine

Until I asked about the meat

It was hare, little rabbits

Tasty and semisweet

It was distressing

Though it would not be

The first time in my life

I ate rabbit meat

But the thought of something so innocent

Getting carved up because of me

Distressed me so much

I could no longer eat

The small creature

With beauty so discreet

Injured and killed in a panic

Just to be a treat

Running and breathing, trying to live

No longer had a heartbeat

It triggered something in me

Unresolved feelings, incomplete

Waldmunt

Dried and warm

Less shaken than before

I walk to my new chambers

To see Bartholomew on his way out the door

We jump and shout

Both of us surprised

I cover myself

And he averts is eyes

I see the curtains on the bed

Along with broaches and costume jewelry

For a single moment

I forget about my nudity

He is halfway out the door, and I call out

"Thank you, Bartholomew."

He pauses a moment, glancing at me

"It's the least I could do."

And out he flees

Leaving me to figure out

How to turn these curtains

Into something I can wear about

I pick them up, and

Fold, tuck, pin, hold

Until they become a flowing garment

Of crimson and gold

And out the room I go

Trying to find my host

Or perhaps a sewing kit

But instead I found a ghost

Waldmunt

Translucent

Ominous

She stares

I am frozen in place

She, frozen in time

Gashes on her chest

I clutch my own breast

The sight of her blood

On her dress

Reminding me of another time

The innocent rabbits for dinner

The woman in front of me

And I, a sinner

Suddenly she's gone

And I am left alone

With my pounding heart

And tears I didn't know I was crying

Bartholomew

I saw her breast

I saw her back

And what I saw

Made my jaw go slack

How many years has it been?

How long since I saw a woman

Bareback, vulnerable

Yet this stranger

Didn't seem to care at all

I ponder and ponder again

Who she is, why she is in my home

When I have to hunt off property

Just to get a bit of food

Yet this woman walks up blandly

As if she had nary a care besides shelter

When her dress was tattered

Yet she herself

Was as calm as can be

I want her here, strange as that may seem

But I told her just a night

And just a night it shall be

What demons she harbors she can deal with alone

For there are far too many ghosts already

In my home

I slump back to the library

Alone, always alone

When Mother comes in through the wall

For once, she appears shaken

"Who is that in the hall?"

She barks, floating to the fireplace

"Just a guest, for a night."

I sigh, feeling more tired than words can describe

"She must go, she cannot be here!

A single night is too long, a night is all she needs!

What will you do, if she doesn't flee?

What if she stays, what if you fall in love?

A child is out of the question, little dove!"

I wince at the nickname from a time much simpler

Mother had given me, before I was a killer

"A child was never on the table, mother

She stays an evening, if she lives through it all

Waldmunt obviously has secrets herself

A woman like that is not one for me

She is on the run, only God knows why

Nothing will happen here, you see

Harboring her for an evening is not do or die

And even if I wanted a mate

I promise no sparks will fly

As that could not happen in a single night, regardless

She'll sleep, and she'll wake, she'll eat, and she'll leave

What else could happen in a time so brief?"

Mother looks at the fire and then back to me.

"You are your father's son

And my dove, blood runs deep."

And she disappears, and that is that

Until I hear the tap

Waldmunt

My heart still races

But my eyes become dry

As I realize that someone like me

Has no right to cry

I walk a while, not sure where I am going

Until I hear whispered words

Being hissed with urgency

I listen at the door

Forgetting all my manners

As anyone who knew me before now knows

I'm no longer a lady

My host and a woman

Speaking with passion

About something I can't make out

Suddenly there is silence

And I gently rap on the door

There is silence only a moment more

When my host answers

"Come in."

I walk inside, looking around

Finding myself in a library

Beautiful and full of literature

But I can't help but feel eerie

As though the room is cold

The source being the man in the center of it all

As if he were a pit so deep

He stole the warmth from me

I walk to him, bowing slightly

And he gestures to the chair across from him

And so I sit to rest my feet

"The curtains suit you, I think

Though it would probably be better

If I had someone here who could sew you

A dress that counts as clothing."

He smiles, and though I don't trust him fully

I can see in his eyes, he is kind

And he is enjoying teasing me

I smile back and look down at my 'dress'

And laugh a bit myself

For it is awkward, with curtains on my body

"Honestly, I still prefer this

To the medieval rags you gave me

I still would like to find a sewing kit

So perhaps it will stay on with more ease."

He opens his hands, palms out

A symbol of surrender

"I am very sorry, Miss Waldmunt

I promise I looked everywhere

But any sewing supplies evaded me

I also must apologize again,

When I brought the curtains to your bed

I thought you would stay longer in the bath

I had no idea you'd come out like that

I swear, I had no intentions to spot you

And…"

He looks down, cheeks red

"I am deeply sorry, I should have knocked

I'm not used to guests, but, no,

I will not give excuses

A lady is a lady and I shouldn't have intruded."

I wave him off

As I have already forgotten it

I don't care whatsoever

About what he has seen or hasn't

I have a thousand other questions

Much more pressing

Do you believe in ghosts?

Who were you just talking to?

Why is there not a single soul in this house,

Aside from me and you?

I hadn't noticed moments before

But the entire room feels warmer

As if the cold that filled the room

Had suddenly evacuated

Leaving me alone with the man

I at first thought had created it

"Do you believe in ghosts?"

I finally ask

Breaking the silence like glass

My host's eyes widen

He stands abruptly

He looks to the fireplace

Then back to me

"I believe in evil

I believe humans were only ever meant to be temporary

Mankind has fallen beyond retrieval

I believe evil lingers

And our own black morals

Will cause our final upheaval

I believe that which cannot be taken back

Will haunt those left behind

And when the trauma overflows

The horror will distort the mind

What is Earth but one massive gravesite?

So much death and ruin

The past is covered in blood

What on earth is truly right?

To answer your question, Miss Waldmunt

I believe in ghosts

And I believe we'll be overtaken by the night."

Waldmunt

We sit in the library

In an uncomfortable silence

His monologue threw me for a loop

But I met it with resilience

I want to stay and talk

And we sit in quiet alliance

For neither of us wants to be alone this night

We look to each other for guidance

So together we face the quiet

Together in asylum

Why do I care of ghosts or the past

When this man feels like an island?

Bartholomew

Though I am not the only ghost in these halls

The things that haunt me cannot make up for

Another human being at all

Someone who is living, who breathes

Living which once seemed so far away from me

We sit in the study, she and I

And though the night dwells on

I am not ready to say goodbye

After a while I stand

And I extend to her my hand

Which she takes with hesitation

Before I walk her to our new station

The ballroom of my home

Where I have not dared to go

For a place so grand and beautiful

Should not exist without another soul

To fill the empty walls

That I was once told

Held the grandest of balls

Silently she follows me

I pull off the sheet

That hid a simple seat

She sits down in to rest her feet

I find the instrument long forgotten

A cello hidden far away

I grab the bow and start to play

Melancholy music fills the room

Waldmunt closes her eyes

Listening to the tune

I play for her and her alone

Until I hear the unearthly moan

Of my mother's ghost, seeing me

Playing for the woman she wants gone

Though our last interaction will be at dawn

I understand why she wants our line to end

But for a moment mother, please let me pretend

That this evening could go on forever

Pretend for a moment longer

That I am a man who can live a normal life

Pretend to myself I am playing for my wife

Mother you are dead

Though the thought of a child fills you with dread

I will continue to play

For tomorrow is the last day

That I will see another living being

Luckily Waldmunt's eyes stay closed, unseeing

I continue to play the cello

The mournful notes still echo

Do not stop me, please

Let this moment stop; freeze

The song will end, and she'll go to bed

I'll etch this moment inside my head

We two are simply broken

We can both tell, though words are unspoken

We both need a simple night

One where we both forget our plight

I can feel she needs this as much as me

So, God, leave us alone, please

Waldmunt

The sound is low, and deep

The tune envelops me

I hear his cries for help in the music

The sound becomes color behind my eyes

The color of something left unsaid

The purplish hue of unsung cries

I know why he brought me here

Why he is playing this can't be misread

He doesn't want to die

I can tell, I can hear it in the song

I can see it in the colors

I can tell, he has been alone quite long

I sit in silence and I hear

The moan of someone very near

My eyes stay shut, for I can't take

Any more surprises on this day

I keep my eyes closed

Letting his soulful music

Take me away

Waldmunt

My sister, oh my poor sister

Lying there in bed

Sobbing, sobbing

My father is enraged

And I, myself

Stand still

I cannot feel anything

All she says is a name

A name

A name

Bartholomew

In the roaring music of my soul

I hear another faint moan

Not of my mother's ghost

Crying for fear of a family line

This one comes from my guest

Whose hands clutch at her breast

As moaning turns to sobs

I throw the cello to the floor

Crouching down by her knees

"I pray, what is wrong?"

I plea

"Your playing was so beautiful,

yet the notes so sad

I'm so very sorry for weeping,

but it reminded me of something bad

Oh, please don't stop on my account

I wouldn't dream it

You play so wonderfully

I fear I am the only one who has seen it

I swear I'm fine, Bartholomew

I only wish I could understand

Exactly what's befallen you."

She finishes her rant with a pitiful little sniffle

Waldmunt dabs her eyes with a corner of her gown

Though the moment is inappropriate, I realize

Her eyes are brown

I hold out my hand and she gently takes it

I pull her up to standing

And our fingers gently knit

"I'm sorry I reminded you of something unpleasant

Perhaps you should retire?"

I gently inquire

She shakes her head yet again

"I wouldn't sleep a wink even if I try."

She says

I try to respond when thunder claps

We both jump together

Filling the gap between our bodies

And I tightly hold her

She does not let go

And I make no offer to

We stand there in the echoes of rain

Two broken people

All by themselves yet again

Her feet shuffle

They shuffle a second time

Suddenly we are dancing rhythmically

To the tune I was playing

We dance together harmoniously

For a moment, hand to God

I could hear singing

For a moment, I swear

There is the sound of musical crescendo

As though the parties of many a year ago

Are all taking place at the same time

We continue dancing, our steps in sync

I wonder if she, too can hear

The sounds of ghosts like me

But her face stays tucked at my chest

Which I don't mind a bit

And for one, beautiful moment, I feel blessed

Staying here alone was not my plan

Though that is what the world needs

For the filth that makes up man

Can have no more of someone like me

I take the woman in my hands

And we dance

We dance

We dance

Waldmunt

I feel in his chest a madness

As though the very essence of this man

Were dipped in darkness

I would not have taken him for it

But I suppose I have been wrong before

He holds me close

And all I want is more

Forget the past, forget it all

Let me stay here longer

How could everything that has transpired

Ever leave someone stronger?

Like the old wives' tale

That every single unfortunate circumstance

Was sent by God to leave you braver

Though I prefer it happenstance

For how could God

Let something so vile

Ever take place

And yet all the while

Those who are truly evil in nature

Go on as though nothing has phased them?

Would He who loves His people let that happen?

If that is the case I forsake Him

Waldmunt

Is there a sin against hating oneself?

I know the sin of suicide

However, is there more of a sin against self-loathing?

The murder of the self seems to me, the last step

In the hatred of the self

Yet is there anything before that, with which God isn't pleased?

There is the sin of standing aside as evil transpires

If that is the case

God is Himself, the greatest sinner

For He knows all the evil of this world

Yet nothing is done by his hand to stop it

Waldmunt

We dance in silence

Though why, I do not know

Perhaps, after the day's trauma

Being held and moving slow

Is precisely what I should have wanted

Perhaps from my sister, or my father

Instead I am in a strange home

One that I do not know

In the arms of a man

I have no reason to trust him

Reason less to dance enwrapped

In his arms as if an old friend

My life has become so abstract

He pulls away suddenly

And that is that

He looks at me for a moment

His lips part ever so slightly

Before he finally speaks

"You should go to sleep."

Shaking my head I plea,

"Don't make me go to bed

There is too much to think of

Too many awful things in my head

So much I wish I could prevent

So much I should have said."

Bartholomew just nods slightly

Before responding,

"You're just a guest

I'm not your keeper

But please know

It would be much safer

For you to go to sleep

Stay in your room

Stay there the whole night

And in the morning

The world will resume

You will be gone

That's all you have to do."

Sighing heavily, I look at him

"What on earth do you know, Bartholomew?

You know nothing of me

And I, nothing of you

You let me into your home

Although, there is no one here

You are all alone

You tell me to stay a night

Then tell me what to do

I swear on my life

If I had had a better day

If everything that has transpired

Were erased

And life could go back to the way I desired

You would still be here, alone

Never again seeing another human soul

I know someone like me

With no more life

No more identity

Has no right to act as if you owe me a favor

I know that because you let me in

You should be no less than my savior

However, you talk of safety

As if there is something in this house

That is out to get me

I swear on my life

Earlier I saw a specter

Though I like you

And obviously I want to stay here

If you are hiding something worse than I

If there is some impending danger

I'd prefer to sleep in a tree tonight

But again, thank you for the dinner."

Bartholomew

There she stands before me

Asking what secrets I hold

With a name I believe false

And garbs that are not clothes

Dusty curtains laced with gold

What is there to this woman?

What makes me want to confess?

Am I truly so starved for human interaction

That I will just take any distraction

It is not like I met her with finesse

I owe her nothing in the world

Yet upon being around a breathing being

All my inhibitions have unfurled

I want to cry in her arms

Tell her of the horrors

That have transpired thanks to my family

Inside the borders

Of this prison I call home

Tell her of my father

Whose only talent in this world

Involved the murder of others

How he haunts this place

And I never had any say

Whether I could stay or go

For my mother's ghost

Insists our line must die with me

For my father's blood runs all too deep

What could my blood offer this world but insanity?

It is part of my heritage

Murder is my family disease

I cannot fight it or escape

This is what my family line has led to

To a man's slow decay

Inside a home where his only companions

Are nothing but ghosts

Inside a home where I waste away

These long, long days

Waiting to die

So that I might help

The world become a better place

"I sit on a foundation of bones."

I do not realize it at first

But the horror is evident in her face

I spoke that aloud

And I feel panic cover me

Like a shroud

"Please don't go."

I hear myself say

As if she ever could stay

I am the only one here who is safe

And as my mother said

The evils of my father's line

Will not stop until I am dead

Waldmunt

I crave the taste of candy

Odd, in this moment

However, whenever I was sad

Sweets came in handy

And though I am in a house

Alone with a man

Who claims to sit on a pile of bones

I just want candy

I want a bath again

I want to curl up in silk

Never dealing with men

Never dealing with anything

Just relax and stop existing

Yes, if only I could stop existing

That would be perfect

Yet life goes on

And that which can afflict

Tends to do just that

So, I suppose I must face this

Face that which I left

I breathe in and finally say

"I won't be leaving

Not this day

I was promised shelter for a night

As you can probably tell

My state of mind isn't right

I don't want to know of the skeletons in your closet

If you have some horrific past

I want none of it

I'll leave in the morning as promised

That was our deal

And I like to think myself honest

If there is such danger here from you

I will go to bed as you requested

So with that I bid you goodnight, Bartholomew."

I walk away from him

From the mysterious man

From his sins

I have my own to tangle with

So much to think about

Though I don't want to

I have to, I have to plan

For I set this all in motion

When all this first began

I must come up with the next step

How to get away

With killing a man

Bartholomew

Through the empty halls I roam

Through the barren veins of my home

Looking to and fro

Feeling emptiness, like a syndrome

Bartholomew

Why did I tell her?

Why did I do that?

What was the point?

I knew she could only stay a night

Perhaps I hoped to push her away

So that I wouldn't get on my knees and beg her to stay

I was born here, and I will die here

In total solitude

I will go to my chambers

And I will be in the clear

No hoping for guests

No wishing for more

I should remember to give up hope

As I have done before

I do not even know what I want from her

Aside from company

What else is there?

I come from a line of people

Whose only joy came

From living in infamy

From pain and torture

My blood is that of monsters

What my family has done

What my father did

Is bloody horror

Servants tied down

And forced to bleed

Wives tied down

Forced to feed

On the bodies of husbands

Madness calls me

As it called my father

Going back in time

Every horrible crime

In living memory

Caused by those

Related to me

And now I am here

With naught but the echoes

Of screams begging forgiveness

When they have done no wrong

There was no hate to the actions

Of those relatives of mine

They heard the screams like a song

And so they sought them out

Creating the music of murder

A song I'm sure the blood lust in us

Hoped would go forever

If I were not such a coward

I should take my own life

Not live here in the dark

Imagining the light

Mother herself wishes I would die

Then, per chance, just maybe

God would let me dignify

The sin of suicide

For my death would spell a safer world

If no more of my kind take breath

Waldmunt

I strip the curtains from my body

Lie in bedsheets deep

Hoping that I will be granted

Just a little bit of sleep

My eyes close and all I see

Is my sister lying in her own bed

Pale as a ghost

Her sweat soaking the sheets

I do not regret my actions

Not a single one

The name repeated is dead

And the world is better for everyone

I instead try to plan

What a woman with no name

No money, no prospects

And a bounty on her head

Should do in the morning

When her temporary bed

No longer welcomes her

What should a woman like that do?

Perhaps keep running

Perhaps turn herself in

Or, maybe, beg her host Bartholomew

To keep her out of sight

Should that kind of woman

Swear on her life

That she will be no burden

That she has no care for

The skeletons he's hidden

Although

That would be a lie

The woman in question

Has killed before

Killed a man who took something

One cannot restore

If Bartholomew's bones

Are, in fact, literal

I do not trust a man who would hurt another

I might just be in the house of a murderer

Which, I suppose, is a bit ironic

Considering my crime may become a bit iconic

As who am I to judge a man

Who has done the same ill as me?

If I am to make a survival plan

I cannot pretend that

The woman I am

Is the lady I used to be

Waldmunt

A scream so loud

It reverberates in my soul

And chatters my teeth

Bursts out and is suddenly gone

As if it had never happened at all

I throw the curtains on

Barely folding them correctly

Running out to the hall

To see what caused the scream

The fabric slips but I just hold it

Running down the halls

Though the drapes continue to be unfolded

I race toward where I believe

The sound might have come from

I pause and wait

For a second scream

Halting at a fork in the corridor

I pull the curtains around me like a towel

Feeling like such a foreigner

A second shriek

Coming from the left of me

And I run again

My knees growing weak

But I must see this to the end

I must know what's happening

I just want the world to make sense again

I follow the sound

Now, now not with my ears

But my soul

As if I'd lived here for years

But, no, that's wrong too

It is more as if my hand were being tugged

By an unknown being

Though I feel no fear

I feel slow, as if drugged

I follow the force

That drags me through

And suddenly, I am at the source

I am faced by two double doors

Deep in parts of the house

I have not yet explored

I reach out my hand

Push open the doors

And all the hollow eyes of the damned

Meet my gaze

And I can't look away

Bartholomew

I lay in bed

Thinking, in dread

Of how long I have to live

How long until I die

Until God might forgive

My being alive

When my mother should perish

By the hands of my father

Yet another miscarriage

Of unholiness that has transpired here

Or my father, murdered

By his own son

Who has since been burdened

With the chore of living to die

I lay still, feeling every ticking second

As the slipping of Waldmunt from me

And loneliness stands at my door to beckon

Me to a different madness

Than that which my father suffered

I make a move to stand

To go to Waldmunt's room

When in comes the specter of Mother

"It is done

We will have no fear

When that woman is gone."

I groan and sit up

"I never feared her

What on earth did you do?"

Mother smirks and claps her hands

With the heir of someone

Accomplishing something so great

No one else could hope to understand

"You told her about the bones

And I showed her to them!

She should be skittering back home

And this will become an unpleasant memory."

I feel nothing at her words, as she is right

I was just an accessory

To her leaving

I lay back down, taking off my shoes

Absorbing the news

She will leave, that was the plan

So, I will simply sleep

I will not get mad, will not weep

Mother was right, she always is

Waldmunt must be gone by now

I'll keep going on without people

Somehow

When my chamber door bursts open

The wood cracking from the force of it

And before me stands Waldmunt

Looking as though she's having a fit

Her curtain garb falling and slipping

And she is crying

She holds a skull in her hand

"Tell me how you do it, man!"

Waldmunt

I see the specter out of the corner of my eye

But I do not care at all

I run to the bed

And in Bartholomew's arms I fall

I sob, oh, god, I sob

He is rigid beneath me

Before he pulls me close

"Do you want some tea?"

He mumbles quietly

I shake my head

Before managing to spit out,

"How have you killed?

How do you take it?

What did they do?

How can you stand to be you?

I want to know, please

Please take the guilt away from me!

He deserved what came to him

And I don't mourn his death

But I mourn the loss of everything else

That left this world with his dying breath."

The words fall out like rain

Full of thunder, lightning, and pain

I cling to him as a drowning man

Clings to the debris of a broken ship

This murderer in my arms

In my mind has formed a partnership

He and I in our evils

I don't care what he did

For I am just like him

A murderer in blood and sin

So I must know how he does it

Killing and living, it doesn't…

How can one not be consumed by guilt?

Waldmunt

We are tangled in each other's arms

And I cannot understand

How the circumstances leading up to this

Threw me in the arms of this man

I know I should have run

Far, far away

But I suppose in terms of common sense

I have none

I had to know how he lives with his actions

But he had no answer

So here we are, two killers

Stewing in emotional abreactions

Bartholomew

I can't help it
I touch her shoulder
Left bare from the slipping
Of the crimson cloth
I feel the warmth
Of another living soul
I can feel the stripping
Of years of solitude
Opening up to something new
A yearning I've buried quite deeply
A feeling much inappropriate for a woman
Who just finished weeping
She turns to me
Eyes red as her 'dress'
"What is to become of me?"
She asks

I sigh heavily before I reply
"I can't tell you
I killed my father for killing my mother,

But not for the other souls he slew

I do not pretend to know

What you did to end up here

But I can tell

That life, you hold dear

I can only tell you to do

What you decide is best for you

I have been listening to the ghost

Of my own mother

Telling me to die

Because the world has suffered

At the hands of half my bloodline

And that no more of me

Should ever see sunshine

I have come to hate her, you see

Hate her and her resentment toward me

For I was the reason the two of them wed

So, I am the reason that she is dead

I often wonder to myself

If perhaps my mother is my worst memory of the house

For nothing is stopping me from stepping

Outside of these walls

But how can I ignore

That which was ingrained in me

Since I was twelve years old?"

Waldmunt

I listen to his story

One of treachery and woes

I reach up, very gently

And kiss him on the nose

He looks surprised

And looks at me in shock

As though he realized I'm something I am not

"Come with me."

I say.

"Come with me outside this home

Learn to breathe another day

I will go, and turn myself in

And you can learn to live again

I only need support

Until I get to the constable's door

Then you can go and get back to living

Without the nagging of your mother

Insisting that your existence is sinning

Maybe you could even meet my family

My sister would love you

For what you've done for me

My father is a gruff man

But I swear, he's really sweet-."

He holds up his hand, to hush me

"Miss Waldmunt, there is no place

Not even here at home

Where someone like me

Should show his face."

Sighing heavily I lightly slap his arm

"Would you do it for my charm?"

I ask.

"No."

He chuckles and takes my hand

"Though, I wouldn't mind it

If you kissed me again."

I snort and turn away

"As if I'd to that for a man

Who won't even leave his house for me!"

We laugh together

As we both know

The other isn't truly bitter

Until a shriek pierces through the room

And we become still

Fearing this may be our doom

Bartholomew

Mother's apparition appears above the bed

She swipes her claws directly

At Waldmunt's head

Screaming she falls back

Away from my mother's attack

I throw Waldmunt from the bed

Screaming at mother to stop

Trying to make her hurt me

In Waldmunt's stead

Why of all times now

Would she decide to kill

When she wanted me dead

Since before I even existed?

"Run!" I scream

Waldmunt limps off

Is her ankle twisted?

"Mother, what are you doing?"

I cry at the specter

Mother bares her teeth

"If she is convincing you to leave

Then I must kill her!"

She flies from the room

Through the wall

Desperately I run to the hall

But there is no sign of her

Or of Waldmunt at all

Waldmunt

My ankle is rolled

I limp as fast as I can

For if I am ever to get out

I must outwit this woman

As I move I feel inside

A strange kind of high

I felt once before

When I was hunting the body

Attached to the name

I learned to abhor

In the name of my sister

Who did nothing wrong

But the name I hate thought

She was too headstrong

The high creeps in

The same as hours earlier

When I held my hunting knife

And the blade became murkier

With the red upon it

The high of hunting him down

The high of sneaking around

Until he was alone at home

When my hands became the color red

And the fool was dead

I feel the high

I feel it

I feel it

I feel

Father

I feel it

I feel it

The bloodlust

I feel

Bartholomew

I run through the halls

Looking for a sign

Of either of them

Ah, forsake this cursed bloodline!

I know in my soul

I'm running out of time

Waldmunt _can't_ be punished

For me or my father's crime

Father

I feel blood

In my fingers

And toes

I feel it

Rushing through

The ankle on this body throbs

I feel pain

I can feel pain again

Sweet, sweet pain

I stumble through the hall

This body is already hurt

So I must try my best to abstain

From causing more damage

Through the wall

I hear the shriek of my wife

Who has desperately been attempting

To end the life

Of our one and only son

And now the woman who could give him

Another chance to fly

Another chance to feel

All of life is precious

At least for my son

At least for my flesh and blood

This woman can get him out

So alive she will have to stay

Suddenly, there is a thud

And I see my wife before me

Her ghostly image

Still dripping with the blood

Of the night she died

"Hello, beautiful."

I say as she charges

And I can tell, she knows my demeanor

For instead of killing the woman

She freezes

"No." She whispers softly

I smile sweetly and step toward her

"If I were you I wouldn't kill me."

If her face could flush it would

Hah, I would kill her again

If only I could

"You're no more, begone!"

She screams

Though she doesn't get closer to me

"The girl's bloodlust gave me power

I was never gone

I was just waiting for the hour

When someone like me came again

What you hated in our boy

What you called my stain

Never penetrated his soul

He would never kill one but me

And yet you could never

Ever let him be free

Begone yourself or I will tell

How your own selfishness

Kept your own child in hell."

She bares her teeth

And makes a move to strike me

When Bartholomew runs in

Halting my reprieve

Bartholomew

Mother is there

Claws ready to strike

And Waldmunt just eyes her

Her body standing, warlike

"Mother, no!

I never had any intention of leaving

So please, I beg of you stop!"

Mother stays in her place

I run over, and mother's face is disbelieving

Taking Waldmunt's hand

I squeeze her cold fingers

"You'll never see her again

Please, oh, please mother!"

There is a chuckle behind me

A sound like no other

I turn around

And see the eyes of my father

"You've only barely grown

If this is the first time

You could tell your mother no."

Shaking, I step back

My father should be gone

Yet here he is

My jaw goes slack

My father is in the body

Of another

Of Waldmunt, my friend

"She is an interesting poppy."

He says, though her lips speak it

"Do you want to know

Why you have been chained to this home?"

"No!"

Mother shrieks and rushes us

I fall back

And in the fuss

Father grabs my hand and runs

Leaving my mother there

And though the timing couldn't be worse

Life was never fair

I'm reminded the last time I touched my father

Was when I stabbed him in the heart

Father

Holding my son's hand in hers

Down the hall we flee

Ignoring the pain in my ankle

That doesn't belong to me

"You have none of my evils, son

If you did, my boy

My time would have come

This woman here is what awakened me

There is none of me in you

So please!

Run from this place

Take the girl with you if you must

Your mother has spent years

Destroying your trust

She didn't want to be alone in death

That is why she tried to keep you here

Until your dying breath!"

Bartholomew follows behind me

He says something very quietly

"Why on earth would I trust you?"

I grit my teeth
"I am your father, Bartholomew!
I would never hurt you!
Your mother was a different story
But I would never harm that which is part of me!"

We continue running
The ankle that is not mine throbbing
When he finally replies
"I will go
Not for my sake
But for hers
For she is the only friend I've ever known
If the only way for her to live
Is for me to live as well
I suppose the world be damned
It can go to hell!"

I grin and run to the door
My son trapped by my wife

No more

Bartholomew

If my father claims

I must escape

Then perhaps if I leave with this woman

He will dissipate

Not unlike a bad scent on the wind

And Waldmunt will be safe

And I can go back to my place

And it will be as if nothing ever happened

I can't, no, I refuse

To believe the woman who raised me

Would keep me in hellish solitude

Simply because she didn't want to be alone

Father… Waldmunt… The one I'm running with

Runs to the front doors, throwing them open

Pushing me outside when I feel a swipe

At my hair, missing by a breadth

Turning I see

Mother's claws

Right next to me

Father opens Waldmunt's mouth to speak

"My son-!"

Then we cross the brink

Of those dreadful double doors

And his voice is again no more

Waldmunt

When I wake the sky is bright

I sit up, curtains spilling off my shoulders

I am nude, but that is the least of my worries

Bartholomew is sitting, back to me

I can tell he silently ponders

I gently touch his back

"What happened?"

I ask

He does not turn to me, no

For he's respecting my privacy

"My father took over you

When we left the house

I suppose he left too

So now I am sitting here

With a woman I don't know

Wondering what I can do

Wondering where to go

Back to my mother

Who may have taken years from my life

Out of fear of being alone

Or go out into the bright

The bright I have not known since I was thirteen

I don't know what to do

Maybe I never did

Maybe life is not something I was meant to see through."

His shoulders shake

And I know he is crying

I press myself against his back, hugging him

For this one moment, no part of me is lying

 I hold him close

I hold him tight

He eventually calms down

After the horrible night

I move over

Sitting by his side

He looks forward

"We don't know each other, you and I."

He says in monotone to which I reply

"Perhaps we don't need to

I am a murderer born in love,

You, an innocent from sin

Or, perhaps I do know you

For we are exact opposites

And for the moment

I just want to make you happy

And I want you to make me forget

Will you help me?"

Waldmunt

We are both unclothed

I rest on his heart

The beat rhythmic and pleasant

I know where I must go

And I believe he does too

But let us lay here

Just a bit longer

Where two people lay bare

Waldmunt

"Are you sure you cannot go with me?"

I ask one last time

Though I know that is just a line

"I will go back to my home

And I will go alone

I will gather my family money

And I will set out on my own

I can't go from leaning on one person

Straight to another, damn it."

His eyes widen as he realizes his curse

"I'm sorry, Miss Waldmunt."

I smile and hold his hand

"I hope we can meet again

Maybe in another land

If I'm ever allowed to breathe fresh air

After I confess my very deliberate blunder."

He smiles and kisses my cheek

And I look down at the creek

I only yesterday used to wash the blood

Of my victim from my hands

"I will go to my family

Then I will go to the law

Setting my fear aside."

He wraps the curtains around me securely

Fastening the fabric with his cufflink

"I will find you, surely

And I will help you as you have me."

We hug one another tightly

A bond created from mutual misery

Bartholomew

I watch her go

No shoes, no clothes

Yet walking with an air of power around her

I thought I could go back home

Pretend this night never happened

But no

I will leave my prison

I will become a true man

And when a better me has risen

We will find each other again

I turn to the mansion

And advance

Epilogue

The constable and his men

Sit around a table

Chatting over their morning meal

In walks their friend with a bag

"What brings you here today?"

They ask

Their friend holds up the sack

"The prisoner wanted something sweet

Before her trial starts

I can't blame the poor thing

Walking in off the street

Admitting to a murder

I know we never would've connected to her

Wearing nothing but drapes

And now come to find she's with-child."

The constable sits back

"I wonder if that's what drove her so wild?"

His friend shrugs

"Perhaps. He seduces her

And then such an incident

As an illegitimate child should occur

In fear and desperation, she stabs him

Nothing I couldn't understand."

Pulling out his pipe

The constable looks thoughtful

"I don't believe that's what happened

You don't kill over something like that

Could you imagine?

I don't believe the child was his

But if she were to claim it is

It could help her case

I believe the baby belongs

To the anonymous donor

Who has paid her way

Given her the best lawyer

To secure her freedom."

The men are silent and thoughtful

As the convict admitted everything to them

But her motive for murder

And her future child's father

"Anyway, what's in the sack?

What kind of sweets does a murderer ask for?"

One of the men asks

"Oh, nothing much."

Their friend replied lightly

"Just some Waldmunt-brand candy."

To keep up with the author and her work, follow her Instagram and Facebook page @lindseybrentonp.

Made in the USA
Middletown, DE
18 April 2019